THE VIEW FROM WORLDSBRIDGE

A Road's Beloved Short Story

ERICA ANOE

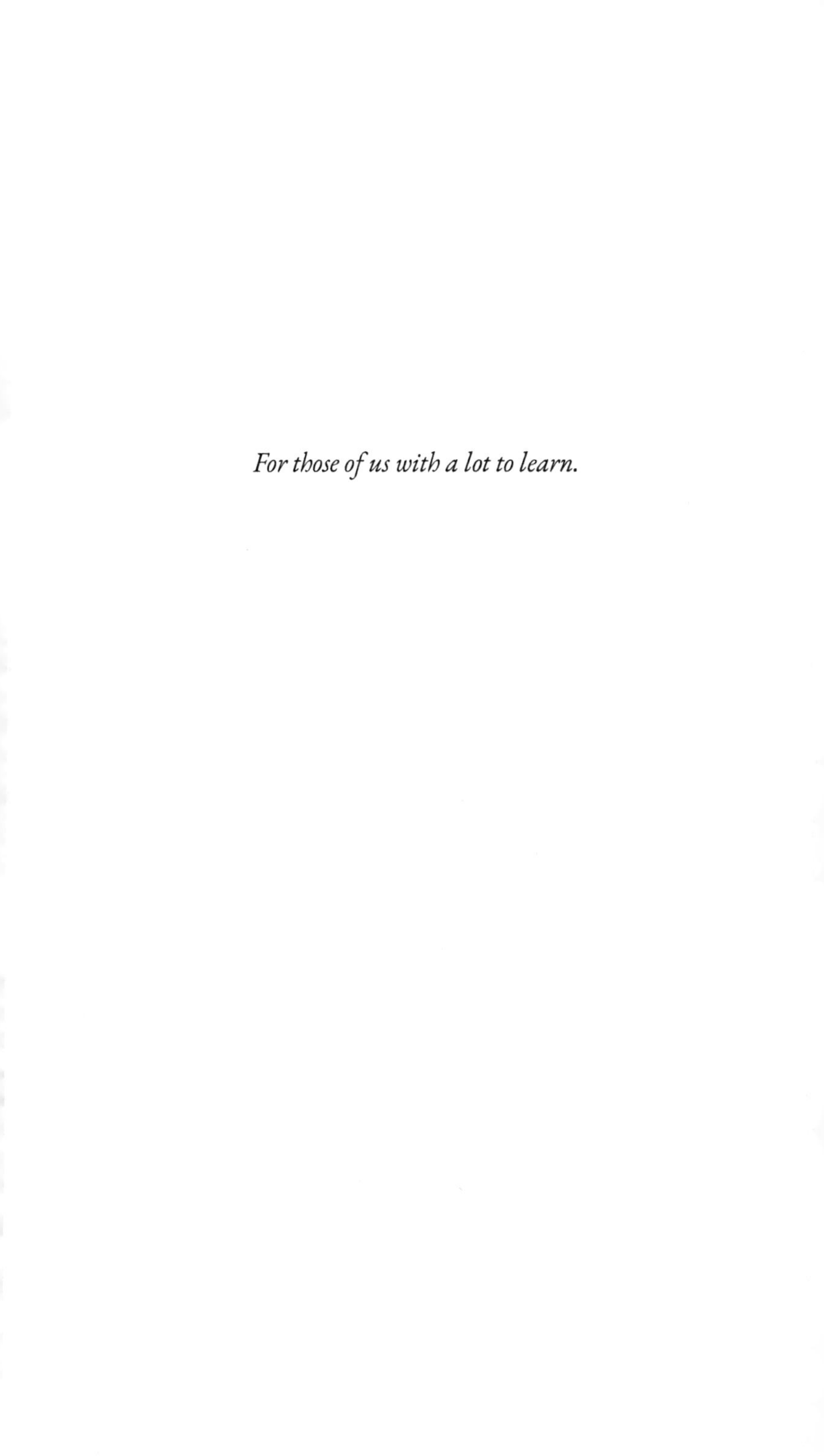

For those of us with a lot to learn.

The very least you can do in your life is figure out what you hope for. And the most you can do is live inside that hope. Not admire it from a distance but live right in it, under its roof.

— Barbara Kingsolver

ONE

Each morning at dawn, Etta stepped out of bed, slipped on her robe – which even after a year still surprised her with its softness – walked to the window of her royal bedchamber and looked out at the view. The skyline of the City sloped gently downward from the high point of the palace, then rose again at the wall. No matter which version of Worldsbridge she looked at, that curving shape was the same, even if sometimes the palace was above the garment district while in this one the smoked meat vendors set up their stalls right outside the palace gates, the scents of their wares sending her stomach to confusion with both the promise of salt and savor and the offputting tang of unfamiliar game.

Beyond the wall was the Road, snaking a meandering route toward the City from somewhere beyond the horizon, its very shape communicating its eternal nature. A mortal being, aware of limited time, would choose a more direct path, but the Road chose interesting ways, paths that wound around haunted hills and through secret places where its chosen Beloved, its eternal travelers, would be sure to find adventure and influence.

Beyond the Road were the beginnings of the Wild. At first, the Wild only manifested in touches among an otherwise tame line of shrubbery along the path, spots where growth took on shapes that seemed more like beings than plants. Farther out, a line of fairly decorous trees sometimes grew fruit of unusually bright and strange colors. But beyond that, the trees crossed their branches like swords and concealed any further revelations from curious eyes.

In the farthest distance to the west, where the world became undefinable, hints of ocean glinted when the sun reached its height in the sky, threads of its seaweed aroma sometimes traveling surprising distances over gusts of strong wind.

The view from her palace in Worldsbridge, Etta had discovered, included City, Road, Wild and Beyond in similar locations no matter how unknown and discomfiting everything else might be. She shivered. As Queen of Worldsbridge, Queen of the Crossroads, the paths available to her were both infinite and limited. She could occupy any world if she could find the way to it – any version of Worldsbridge that ever had or could ever exist. But she must be bound to the City, for any attempt she'd made to leave simply landed her in another version of Worldsbridge.

Etta tugged the robe tighter around her body and breathed the air of this latest world. It resembled the Worldsbridge she'd grown up in, but slight changes like the nature of the meat set her more on edge than when she found herself in utterly alien versions of the City. In some ways, she'd felt more comfortable in the version of Worldsbridge where the people had tried to burn the palace with her inside it, for example, or the one where the Road's Beloved had become poachers and bounty hunters and walked about adorned with gruesome trophies. At least in those places, she'd known in her bones never to let down her guard. Here, she was disarmed by the false resonance with her childhood, only to have a wall of anxiety snap suddenly in place whenever something reminded her she wasn't actually at home.

She was startled from those memories by movement on the Road far beyond the wall – though she didn't admit this to herself, she checked the view regularly to watch for just this sort of movement. *Piper,* she thought, the name accompanied by a wash of complicated feelings – freedom, pleasure and loss.

Etta leaned so far out the window that she had to catch herself on the sill to prevent herself from toppling over. In the distance, she could just make out a figure on foot. Of course, it wasn't Piper, Beloved of both Etta and the Road. The Road had taken Piper from Etta the first time they'd crossed one of the bridges between worlds that gave the city its name. Etta didn't know the reason for the separation, and she had no idea where Piper had wound up. Much as she might wish for it, there was little chance Piper would simply walk up to this version of Worldsbridge now. Besides, Etta would have recognized Piper's silhouette anywhere, and this wasn't her.

Sighing, Etta hauled herself back into the bedroom. Its richly appointed furnishings had lost their luster for the moment, as had the breakfast of eggs and buttered leeks that had been delivered by a servant while Etta looked out at the view. She picked up her plate absently and forced down the meal one bite at a time, despite how thick it felt in her mouth. Whether or not she wanted the rich food at the moment, she'd grown up too poor to let it go to waste.

Etta moved toward the closet and started when she realized the servant who'd delivered the breakfast hadn't left. The woman stood beside the doorway, hands tucked as tightly behind her back as her hair was tucked into her cap. "May I help you?" Etta asked, setting the plate down and then unable to resist the urge to adjust it on its tray. She still felt odd around people who expected her to act like a Queen – she still wasn't sure how a Queen was supposed to act.

"Your Majesty, it is I who should ask that question of you."

"Of course," Etta murmured. "What is your name?"

"Theresa."

"How long have you worked in the palace?"

"Since yesterday."

Etta raised an eyebrow.

"The Chancellor hired me and many others when we spotted you approaching from the horizon."

"How did you know who I am? Many people approach Worldsbridge – someone is approaching now – and not all of them are Queen."

"The Herald came before you. He has been sharing his maps and telling your story. He gave us the signs by which we would know you."

"Who is this Herald?"

"A man, a Road's Beloved like yourself. Tall, pain in his eyes, marked almost everywhere, though he follows a book rather than the path the Road has given him. His skin is burnt as if not used to the sun. He walked with a limp and had bindings around his ankle and elbow. The way seemed to have been hard for him."

Etta began to pace. She knew who this person had to be. "Please," she told Theresa, "sit down. There's some tea left from the breakfast you brought. You should have some."

Theresa twisted her hands before her body. "Ma'am, I'm not sure one such as me should be talking with you this way."

Etta couldn't help rolling her eyes. She placed her hands on Theresa's shoulders, and the servant flinched away. *You don't know the details of this place or what has happened in this woman's life,* Etta reminded herself. *You may think you do, but things here could be very different from anything you imagine.*

She let go of the other woman and backed away, holding up her hands to show she wasn't a threat. "I'm sorry," Etta said. "I shouldn't have touched you without permission."

Theresa bit her lip. "Ma'am, you are Queen. I think you can touch me however you wish."

Etta's stomach turned with revulsion. "I'm not sure how you've been treated in the past or how things generally are in this City, but I don't wish to touch you – *ever* – in any way you don't wish me to. Do you understand?"

Theresa nodded, but Etta needed to be sure.

"If I do anything to you that you don't want, you must tell me. Please."

"I'll try, Your Majesty."

"Good." Etta took a deep breath. She'd wanted to pull Theresa to a seat and tell her not to worry about the differences between them. She'd wanted to say she'd grown up just like Theresa and had only been Queen for a short time. But she saw now that anything she said, any movement she made, carried an air of authority that she needed to be careful with. The idea made her miss Piper deeply, sharply, right at the pit of her stomach. Etta had never felt lonelier than realizing now how she could no longer be herself. If Piper were here, there would have been relief. At least at night when the bedroom door was closed, they could have–

Etta cut off the thought, knowing she couldn't afford to go down that path. She needed to focus her attention on the woman before her.

"Theresa," Etta tried again. "If you don't wish to speak with me any further, you may go back to your duties. However, if you are willing, I would like to talk with you, and if you aren't used to being listened to because of who you are – I promise I will."

Slowly, Theresa nodded.

"Now, which would you prefer?"

Theresa glanced over her shoulder as if someone might be watching her and then stole to the table where the remains of breakfast sat, her movements furtive and her gaze downcast. She poured herself a cup of tea with a shaking hand. Etta wanted to reach out and steady the hand, but she twisted her fingers in her robe to prevent the instinctual movement. She waited until Theresa had hesitantly stirred a sugar cube into the tea.

"I hate to give you just the scraps, but there's a biscuit I haven't eaten yet."

Theresa's dark eyes flickered toward and away from Etta. She took the biscuit.

"I'm glad you stayed," Etta said, smiling gently. She returned to the window and sat on the sill, not wanting to crowd Theresa. The woman was fairly young, maybe early twenties. She had the beauty of a flower struggling up between stones. Her servant's dress was plain but new, and she looked good in it. The anxious watchfulness of her gaze and the jumpiness of her mannerisms held a strange attraction. They called up the urge to soothe and care for her, and Etta wondered if Theresa had yet learned to use that quality to her advantage.

She watched Theresa eat the biscuit, then spoke again. "Your description of this Herald was very detailed. How did you see him?"

"Everyone saw him. He got to the city and asked to talk to the Chancellor. With all those marks he had on him, we knew it had to be important. The guard let him in. People talked about him constantly from the moment he arrived. We're used to the Road's Beloved who carry goods back and forth between us and the Wildfolk to the north and the ones who bring fish up from the sea and others who come with messages from time to time, but you could tell right away that he was something different. After he talked to the Chancellor, he wanted to address the city, so we all gathered below the palace balcony to hear him speak. Of course, we were curious what he'd have to say, but we also just wanted to see him and his marks."

Etta nodded. This tracked with the way she'd understood Road's Beloved growing up. She remembered the moment she'd first seen Piper, her instant and absolute fascination with the markings on her skin – though as Piper had said, what was visible with clothes on were only a fraction. Etta had been overwhelmed by the quantity of Roads that Piper's markings represented, covering almost every inch of her as they did. When they made love, she used to try to trace the lines with her fingertips as if following a maze, but she never found the beginning or end of them. Her life was divided into the time before Piper had arrived, when Etta had been an ordinary member of the City Guard, and after Piper had arrived, when Etta stepped onto the path she walked now. In the time before Piper, she'd have flocked to see a well-marked Road's Beloved along with the rest of the citizenry, just as Theresa had.

She gestured for Theresa to continue.

Theresa wiped the corner of her mouth, then ate the crumb she'd picked off her lip. "He told us you were coming and we needed to be ready. He explained to us what the name Worldsbridge means. He showed us maps he had drawn. He explained about other worlds. He said there is always a ruler of Worldsbridge and that the ruler is supposed to travel from one world to another and care for us all."

Etta's eyes widened. "Did he happen to say anything about how that's supposed to work?"

Theresa's forehead wrinkled. "Don't you know? You're the Queen."

"I haven't been Queen very long," Etta admitted. "I'm still... learning the territory, I guess you could say." She glanced out the window and saw that the person approaching had gotten closer. She could make out the shape well enough to see a tall man carrying little. She nodded toward the figure. "What do you do when a Road's Beloved arrives?"

"We honor them, trade with them, listen to their messages, give them our messages to carry. You probably don't know how this is, since you're Queen and can go anywhere you like, but when you live in the City – I don't mean to complain. It's a big place, and there's a lot here to look at, things to buy, people to talk to." Theresa ran the fingers of one hand back and forth across the lacy tablecloth where she'd set down Etta's breakfast. Her other hand fiddled with something in the pocket of her dress.

She said, "It's just that, you don't really know what's outside the city walls. You only know what you can see if you can get somewhere higher up. Or the things the Road's Beloved say when they arrive." She laughed softly. "You know, there's people who say fish don't really come from the ocean. The idea of all that water stretching out for miles – maybe it's just a made-up story. How would we know if there's an ocean or if there are dragons or elves or people who can live in the wilds or other worlds and other places called Worldsbridge? All we know is what people like you say to us." There was an edge of anger in her voice that caught Etta's attention.

Etta shifted her position subtly away from the window to avoid any potential for unpleasant accidents. She wore only her robe and hadn't thought to carry a weapon from the bed to the window – the unfortunate effect of relaxing when she felt like she was home – but her City Guard reflexes turned on and she lowered her center of gravity and watched Theresa's movements more closely. Etta wondered what she had in that pocket, but she kept the expression on her face easy.

"You know, Theresa, I actually can't go anywhere I like. I grew up in a place very like this city, feeling very much like what you just described. I guarded the gates of the City and I was often there when the Road's Beloved came. It was always exciting to watch them arrive, shake off the dust of the Road and hang their shoes up at the city gate. I wasn't a Road's Beloved until a year ago when a woman named Piper came. I certainly wasn't Queen. Until I became a Road's Beloved, the magic that divides City from Road and Road from Wild and Wild from City kept me inside the city walls, too, much as I wondered what it would be like to cross that barrier."

Theresa cocked her head at Etta, her expression changing. "But you're the Queen now."

"Well, yes. I still can't go anywhere I want. You know that the markings on a Road's Beloved represent all the roads you have ever walked – or will ever. You can cross the barriers, but you can't simply go where you please." Etta held out one arm, showing the inside of her wrist. Just over the place where her veins came closest to the surface of her skin was a thick black X, a mark that had appeared there the day she'd met Piper, when the Road itself appeared to her and took her by the hand. She sometimes thought she remembered his thumb brushing her just there. She touched it with a fingernail.

"This represents Worldsbridge," she told Theresa. "And the lines that grow outward from it represent the bridges from here to other worlds. But if you look closely at my markings, you'll see they all come back to here. I can leave any given Worldsbridge, but as soon as I cross into another world, I arrive at a new Worldsbridge. In the year since I became Queen, I've been to 67 versions of this city. It's a sort of freedom, and I'm grateful for it. But–" she swallowed, Piper never far from her thoughts. "It's not the same as being able to go anywhere I want, see anyone I want. I think being Queen means having responsibility, being bound to a place and its people."

Theresa stared at Etta long and hard. "You're not like he said you would be. It's hard to believe…"

Etta's heart sped its beating. "What exactly?"

Theresa was silent, and Etta approached a few steps cautiously. She noticed Theresa's hand still in her pocket, clenched. "Theresa, I'll admit I'm not sure where your loyalties lie. But I'm asking you, as a favor to me, to tell me what you know. What story did this Herald tell?"

"I have a duty, my Queen, to the Chancellor and to this version of Worldsbridge and to every other world besides."

"And what exactly is this duty?"

Theresa hesitated and reached for her teacup. Her free hand still shaking, she dropped the teacup and it shattered. Etta approached to help, but kept an eye on that pocketed hand.

Sure enough, when she got within range, Theresa's hand emerged from the pocket holding a slim knife. She sliced upward with it, but Etta dodged out of the way. Theresa lunged, sending her chair clattering to the floor beside the shattered teacup. Etta caught her wrist and squeezed, trying to make her drop the knife.

Theresa sprang forward even farther, her free hand clawing Etta's eyes. Etta cried out and fell back, giving Theresa the opportunity to pull away from her grip.

Eyes tearing up, Etta felt for any object she could use to bludgeon, slice or shield. Her hand found its way to her now-empty breakfast plate, which she flung in Theresa's direction to open space between them. It crashed against something, but it did buy Etta a few seconds. She swiped her eyes clear with the back of her hand and got hold of a ceramic lamp from beside the bed, the oil still warm from the flame Etta had lit in it before dawn broke. She shifted her grip on the solid object and stared Theresa down.

"I'd like to know what duty you think you have and what it has to do with killing me. You said much of what you know about the world are stories the Road's Beloved tell. What did this Herald say?"

Theresa panted from the exertion, her back against the door to the royal bedchamber. "He said a woman came to Worldsbridge with her lover, long ago, both Road's Beloved, and locked the rightful King into a dungeon and took his throne. They kept him in that dungeon for many long years, preventing him from traveling between the worlds and caring for his people in other places."

Etta scoffed but suppressed any other reaction, hoping Theresa would continue talking.

After a moment, she did. She still held the knife, but circled her wrist as if she could still feel Etta's fingers squeezing. "He said the two women took his place without care for the damage they did to everyone in those other worlds by leaving them without their rightful ruler. He said eventually the rightful King escaped. That's when the women decided to travel the bridges and visit the other worlds in the domain. They wanted to find him and prevent him from taking shelter among his subjects in another version of Worldsbridge. That's why, he said, we should expect you, even if we hadn't seen a King or Queen of Worldsbridge in more than a generation."

"That's quite a story." Etta flared her nostrils in irritation. "Did this wise Herald also happen to be the rightful King of Worldsbridge?"

"So he said."

"Are you going to try to kill me again?"

"I'm afraid I have to." Theresa gave a cry and launched herself at Etta, knife aimed for the gut. Etta blocked the blow with a forearm but got the back of her arm slashed open in the process. She followed the block by hitting the lamp against Theresa's ribs, knocking the wind from her.

Pressing her advantage, Etta flung Theresa onto the bed and followed her down, pinning her to the mattress. Holding

Theresa in place with her full body weight, Etta used her left forearm to restrain Theresa's knife hand. With her right hand, Etta tried to wrest the knife from the other woman's grip. Theresa writhed and grunted beneath her, reminding Etta of more pleasant horizontal experiences. The memory of Piper was interrupted by Theresa's teeth sinking into Etta's forearm, preventing her from getting hold of the knife.

"Damn it, woman," Etta said, yanking her arm free and feeling the sting of the bite marks. "I want to talk to you."

"It won't do any good to talk to you," Theresa said, struggling.

"How do you know?"

The servant sighed and was still for a moment. Surprised by the change, Etta looked her in the eye. Theresa's gaze was surprisingly soft for a person who was trying to kill her. "If I talk to you," Theresa said, "I might listen to you. Then I won't do what I've been hired to do. That will have consequences."

"Theresa, I know you have no reason to trust me," Etta said. It was starting to feel difficult to talk while holding the woman down. "But I wish you would trust me, just for a little while. Please."

"Trust you to do what?"

"Trust me with the truth. Trust that I might be able to help with whatever consequences you're afraid of."

"How could you? You don't know anything. The Chancellor's the one who rules here. When the rightful King arrives, he and the Chancellor will throw you in the dungeon, and then we'll set things right around here."

"I see," Etta said. If she thought about the larger picture of it all, she felt foolish and out of her depth. She'd handled her arrivals differently at different times. The first time she'd crossed a world's bridge, she'd been heartbroken at the loss of Piper and determined to throw herself into her duties as a means of distraction. The people said they'd been waiting for her, and they had helped her. Most of her time in that place had been spent in the library learning about the structure of the worlds.

She wanted to say there had been no time to learn governance, but unfortunately, she couldn't while being honest with herself. For a long time, she'd wanted to find Piper more than anything, and she'd traveled quickly from one world to another without staying long enough anywhere to understand how to be Queen. Sometimes she'd announced herself as Queen at the gate. Other times, she'd tried to be in the city without being noticed and brought to the palace. It was true that recently she'd encountered more hostility, but she hadn't thought anything of it – it was impossible to know what was usual or unusual as she traveled through ever-changing worlds.

The moment she'd taken on the role of Worldsbridge's Queen had felt triumphant and inevitable. Casting out the mad King Willburn and sitting in the throne the first time had been the right thing to do, and she'd done it. The Road had placed her there, crowned her. But the Road had not told her what she ought to do next. That, Etta understood, was not the Road's way.

Beneath her, Theresa had gradually given up the fight. "What are you going to do to me?" she breathed. Etta again became uncomfortably aware of how long it had been since she'd last shared a bed with Piper.

"I don't know," she said. "I'd like to let you go. I did tell you I wouldn't touch you without your permission. But I can only let go of you if you let go of the knife."

The rise and fall of Theresa's chest as she recovered from her exertions transferred the rhythm of her breathing to Etta. Theresa's forehead wrinkled as if trying to work out a complex problem. "Please don't hurt me," she whispered. Her hand opened, and the knife fell softly to the mattress.

Etta collected it and stood up from the bed, holding onto the knife to keep Theresa at arm's length if need be.

"Who are you really?" Etta asked. "If the Chancellor hired you yesterday and you're not simply here to bring me eggs?"

Theresa sat up slowly, rubbed her ribs and then her wrist, and shrugged. "I'm not much of anybody really. I'm someone they thought could get close to you."

"You're a servant I wasn't supposed to notice. You were going to stab me in the back while I ate my eggs."

"Something like that. We expected you to be with someone else. When you came alone, the Chancellor said I might be able to... distract you."

Etta bit the corner of her lip, thinking she might not have been able to hold out if Theresa had given that a real try. She'd been terribly lonely, and her hopes of finding Piper had been fading. "Why didn't you?"

Theresa hesitated. "You just weren't what I expected. Something about the whole thing seemed wrong. I wasn't sure what I ought to do or how to do it or when to start – and I wasn't sure if I wanted to."

"What did they promise you if you accomplished this?"

"Food for my family. Freedom for my brother – he's been in the palace dungeon since he got caught trying to steal to help us. Work in the palace so we won't have to go hungry anymore."

"Those are pretty attractive offers."

Theresa nodded sadly. "Now I've ruined it all," she said. "I haven't done what they wanted me to. But I tried to do it, so I'm sure you–"

Etta waved the thought away. "You'll have a chance to redeem yourself."

"What do you mean?"

"I need to know the rest of the plan. What was supposed to happen after you stabbed me in the gut?"

"The Chancellor said to go to him and he'd see to my reward."

Etta set the knife down on an end table and went to sit beside Theresa. She reached out to take her hand but paused mid-air, waiting to see if the woman accepted the gesture. When she did, Etta let their hands rest gently on her thigh. "I'm afraid your 'reward' might not have turned out to be food at all."

"I thought of that, but what choice did I have? They'll execute my brother soon, and then where will we be? I had to try."

"And after the Chancellor slid a knife between your ribs in payment for spilling my blood – I suppose the Herald would return to Worldsbridge and resume his 'rightful' throne."

"I think that was the idea. But Your Majesty – I'm sure I'm not the only one with a mission like this. The Chancellor hired a lot of people the day he hired me."

Etta squeezed her hand. "I suppose we'll have to be on guard."

"We?"

"If you're willing to help me."

"How?"

Etta raised an eyebrow. "And for what? You should ask that, too."

"For what, then?"

"For your brother's freedom. Which you'll know I can grant because the first thing we're going to do is get him out of the dungeon."

"How will we do that?"

"I am the Queen of Worldsbridge," Etta said, getting to her feet and opening her wardrobe so she could change out of her robe. There were many fine outfits inside, but after some searching, she was able to find an outfit for riding that consisted of pants and a shirt rather than a multitude of skirts. She used a scarf to bind her still-bleeding arm.

"Not only am I Queen, I am also a Road's Beloved," Etta said as she tugged on the pants. "I have much to learn, but I know the Road tends to make sure that its Beloved have a way."

Etta returned Theresa's knife, then searched quickly for one of her own. She'd been a fool to go unarmed at all. Once she found this new weapon, she picked it up and resolved to ensure she was never again without it.

Theresa went to open the door, but Etta stopped her, searching the room instead, feeling along the stone.

"What are you doing?" Theresa asked.

"They may be watching for you to come out that door. If we leave it closed, they may think you're still distracting me. I'm looking for an alternate route."

"I don't think there's anything like that here," Theresa said, just as Etta found a hidden panel and slid it open, revealing a dark stairway down. She'd learned that the Road's gifts to the Queen of the Crossroads included the ability to find and open doors.

Etta smiled at her. "You were saying?" She gestured downward.

Two

The dungeons smelled of human misery in the form of sweat and blood and excrement. As a member of the City Guard, Etta had at times sent people here, but she'd believed conditions were better in her version of Worldsbridge. Perhaps that had been true in her version of Worldsbridge, or perhaps she'd simply wanted to believe it.

Their stairway opened onto an odd alcove outside the view of the guards. Smoke from grease-soaked rush candles filled the air and stung Etta's eyes. People gave low moans as if suffering from nausea, recovering from beatings or both. Shadows gathered in Theresa's face, and Etta resisted the urge to comfort her. "Lead the way," Etta murmured. "I suspect he won't be far."

Theresa pressed her lips together and stepped forward. She held her knife in front of her as she walked. In a scabbard at her hip was a short sword intended for her brother.

They passed one empty cell, and then Theresa let out a quiet sob. "Matthew!"

The person in the cell got to his feet. Etta was relieved to see that he seemed able-bodied and not too ill. He must have been caught stealing recently.

Theresa turned toward Etta. "How will we get him out? The cell is locked."

"That's only the way the guards use. There are other ways in." She touched a bar of the cell, knowing her words to be true. Sure enough, she felt the bar rattle loosely in her hand. "This is actually a door," Etta said, her Road-given power making it so. The cell opened to her, and they gestured for Matthew to come out.

He must have been a younger brother – he looked right on the cusp between boy and man. He had Theresa's dark eyes and a smattering of hair on his chin and cheeks. The hair on his head was thick and unruly. He wore rags, and Etta made a mental note to find him something better.

Theresa whispered quick introductions and a brief explanation of how they had come to rescue him.

"Your Majesty," Matthew said, bowing his head with a touch of insolence. "I don't mean to doubt your powers – it's incredible that the cell opened. But how are we going to get past the guards?"

"The thing is," Etta said, "I believe I remember that there's a passageway that leads straight from the palace dungeon to the guard tower at the city walls. It's a convenient way to bring prisoners here when they shouldn't be paraded through the streets."

She dropped to her knees and felt on the floor for the handle of a trap door that she knew must be there – in some version of Worldsbridge, and therefore in this one.

"I've never heard of such a thing," Theresa said.

Matthew nodded. "I'm afraid they always bring prisoners in through the hallway over there."

"Found it," Etta said, swinging the trap door open with a sense of pride. She didn't wait for them to stop staring before disappearing down it. Etta might not yet be a good Queen, but today she was making the best use she could of the things she did know how to do.

The trap door led to a wide passage with smooth floors and walls lined with lit torches.

"What is this place?" Theresa asked, her head swiveling in arcs that matched the graceful curves of the supporting beams.

"It's the passage we need to take to the guard tower," Etta replied, beginning to walk.

As they moved, Etta studied Matthew's stride, looking for signs of injury. He moved well enough, but she felt some pangs of guilt about what he'd likely been through.

"You're the two people I know I can trust in this city," Etta told them. "If I could avoid asking anything more of you right now, I would, but I'm afraid I need your help. Are you with me?"

"Do we have a choice?" Theresa asked.

"With me – with the Road and any of the Road's true Beloved – you always have a choice. The very nature of the Road is choice. If you don't wish to accompany me to the guard tower, turn and walk the other way down this passage."

"Going back to the dungeon isn't much of a choice," Matthew said.

Etta stopped walking. "You'll find the passage goes wherever it makes sense for it to go. Perhaps to the place you live? Or a lover's house?"

"How is that possible?"

"Your sister told you who I am. Why don't you believe it?"

"They've been talking about it since the Herald came, even in the dungeon," Matthew said. "The false Queen, the reason our ruler hasn't come to help us."

Theresa shook her head. "I don't think that story's true."

"How do you know? You've known her for all of one morning."

"And how long have we known the Herald? Look how the city opens for her. As if perhaps she's the rightful ruler?"

Etta smiled, warmed by Theresa's defense of her. "If you come with me to help, I will be grateful and reward you as best I can. If you decide to leave, I will not blame you. You are free to choose."

"We're with you," Theresa said loudly.

"I appreciate that you are," Etta replied, but turned to Matthew. "And you? Your sister cannot speak for you in this."

"Yes," he said. "I suppose I am."

"I'll try not to let it become a fight, but it may," Etta told them. She led the way toward the city walls.

THREE

It had begun this way, and now here Etta was again - inside the guard tower, watching a Road's Beloved approach Worldsbridge. She recalled how she'd often talked to Piper about circles and how they played into her theories of the nature of the Road.

She stood behind the gate of the city, watching as the self-proclaimed Herald came toward Worldsbridge. Theresa stood to her left and Matthew to her right, all of them better armed now thanks to the supplies in the guard tower. Behind them were a line of guards who Etta also believed she could trust – guards who hadn't been hired by the Chancellor yesterday, people who got a particular wistful look in their eyes when they looked out at the Road or at the mark on Etta's wrist.

The man was unmistakable now that she could see him clearly. The marks of the Road covered his skin almost as thickly as they did Piper's, his maps much more expansive than Etta's. Still, Etta knew that this man had betrayed the Road and allowed the maps and gifts it had given him to die. She stroked the X on her wrist, comforted now by the gentle contrast of the thick, dark mark against her red-brown skin.

She still thought about Piper constantly, but she resolved to do better at being Queen despite her heartbreak and individual concerns. Theresa and Matthew weren't the only two people who'd been starving in some version of Worldsbridge while Etta hopelessly chased her lost lover.

As she watched the Herald arrive at the gate and remove his shoes to shake away the dust of the Road, her mind again returned to the day she'd first seen Piper undertake the same ritual. *I have to let you go,* Etta thought. Maybe she was right that the Road loved circles and would one day bring her and Piper back together. But she didn't know for sure and she couldn't allow the hope to distract her any longer.

"City of Worldsbridge," the Herald proclaimed. "Your rightful King has arrived, and I demand entry."

Etta reached out to the gates. The sun-warmed wood fooled her with its sense of familiarity. How many times had she pressed her palms against gates such as this in past years, wishing she could pass through them, leave the City and discover the Road and the Wild beyond it? These gates, however, were not the gates she'd grown up with. They sprang open at her touch and brought her face to face with the unworthy ruler she'd deposed with the help of Piper and the Road itself.

He'd changed and grown stronger since she'd last seen him – he was no longer a weakened husk hiding from sun, Road and responsibility in the throne room of the palace at Worldsbridge. Still, the twist of his thoughts was visible in the madness of his expression, the cruel and wild eyes and the curl of his lips when he saw her. As Theresa had said, it seemed his paths had been hard on him. His left ankle was bound with dirty cloth and he walked with a pronounced limp.

"Hello, Willburn," Etta said. "I wish I could say it was good to see you, but it appears you're trying to have me killed."

"I've made my choice, as you said I must when you took my realm from me," the mad king replied, his voice still dry and thin.

"And your choice is?"

"You see it before you. I have been walking, and my maps are becoming true. How else do you think I found my way to this world just before you?"

"I'm pleased you're restoring your gift, but you could use true maps for a better purpose."

"Like you? You think you're better than me just because you move more? What are you doing for the people of this or any Worldsbridge?"

"Not enough," Etta said, drawing herself up tall. "But I swear by the Road and the marks it has given me that I will do better."

Willburn snarled and looked past her to the guards. "You remember when I came and spoke to you from the palace balcony, don't you? This is the woman I spoke about, the one who kept me captive for many years and prevented me from coming to be your King. You must arrest her!"

Etta did not glance behind her to see if any of them were moved by his appeal. She'd chosen people she believed had discernment, and if it wasn't evident who she was compared to Willburn when they stood face to face like this – well, in that case, maybe Etta wasn't who she thought she was after all.

However, as Etta expected, no one moved. She shook her head and spoke gently to the mad king. "Willburn, the only one who kept you captive was yourself. The day you met me was the day I set you free to walk the Road again. I didn't take anything from you that you hadn't already taken from yourself."

"And the other woman?" Willburn asked. "The pretty one? Where has she gone?"

She sighed, unsurprised that Willburn had asked a question that would sting. "The Road had a different path for her to walk. You know the Road can be cruel – Piper and I never denied that."

"You call me the mad king behind my back, but you're the mad one," Willburn hissed. "That you would serve the Road when it uses us and tosses us away, when it promises everything and costs everything and gives nothing."

"I won't tell you things you already know about Roads and journeys and the nature of rewards," Etta said. "What I will tell you is something I have told you before. I am Queen of this Crossroads, the Queen of Worldsbridge. Its doors and ways are open to me as they are to no other. Even if these guards obeyed you and arrested me, there are no walls anywhere in Worldsbridge that can hold me in."

"Lies," Willburn hissed. "False Queen. I am the true ruler of this place."

"You were," Etta said. "But ruling, like traveling, is about making choices, and by refusing to choose and refusing to act, you abdicated your throne years before I took it. I will prove it to you."

"Try."

"It is simple," Etta said. "Worldsbridge opens itself and its secrets to its true ruler. Theresa and Matthew have seen some proof of how this works for me, and I can offer much more to any other who needs to see. But Willburn, you poor lost Beloved of the Road, I am about to close this door to you and you will not be able to open it and come in."

Etta reached for the gate, but before she touched it, Willburn fell to his knees before her. "Please," he said. "I am so tired. I have nowhere to go, no home except this place. You can't do this to me. You must take me in. I can help you. I know many things you have not yet learned. I read many of the books in the library, extracted many secrets from the Road's Beloved who came through the city while I ruled."

"You mean you forced them to tell you things when you tortured them to death, and you stole their skin for maps after having them killed."

The people around and behind her gasped, but Willburn did not deny it. Instead, he said, "You would be a fool to lose what I have to offer."

"I'll take my chances and make my choices," Etta said. "You have not treated this place as a home, and therefore it will be your home no more." She did touch the gates then and slammed them shut, and all who were there to witness it saw that, though Willburn remained outside the wall begging, screaming, crying and cursing for three days and three nights, the great city obeyed Etta's command and did not let him in.

Etta, however, did not spare him the time. She turned her back to the gate and the Road and Wild beyond it so she could face Theresa and Matthew and the guards who had come with her. For the first time since she'd taken the throne, she truly felt like a queen. "People of Worldsbridge," she said, "I am a new Queen, but I swear to you now that I will spend every day and night learning to be a better Queen – to be *your* Queen." Those gathered there saw her for what she was and believed her. They fell to their knees and swore their loyalty to her.

And Queen Etta, Queen of the Crossroads, Queen of Worldsbridge, the place where all Roads meet, the nexus of worlds, bade them rise and then led them back to the palace to deal with the Chancellor.

Author's Note

This is the first Road's Beloved story I've written without Piper making an appearance, but I always knew that this world and this story were bigger than one person. Though Etta and I both feel Piper's absence, I'm glad to have learned more about who Etta is and what it means for her to be Queen. I'm glad to see her stepping into the spotlight.

When Etta first appeared in "Queen of the Crossroads," my first Road's Beloved story, she was "faceless hot City Guard." She didn't have a name until I realized she needed one. Her original purpose was to make Piper look cool – a character who would go to Piper when Piper crooked her finger and be suitably impressed. Piper treated her that way, too.

Etta, however, had other ideas. She wanted to hold onto Piper because they had a real connection, but she also refused to be an insignificant character. I learned from this, and so did Piper. Everyone is and should be the hero of their own story, and Etta was too deep and interesting to be discarded as "faceless hot City Guard."

By the end of the first Road's Beloved story, Etta became

Queen of Worldsbridge. Piper never forgot the lesson, and in every story I've written about her since, she's been more careful with people's hearts, and she's remembered not to write anyone off as momentary entertainment. You never know a person's larger destiny, and you can count on the Road by its very nature to use a chance encounter for a grand purpose.

As a writer, I learned that I don't want to write throwaway characters. Etta became so interesting to me as she expanded and took her true place in the storyline. By the time I started "The View From Worldsbridge," I had learned my lesson. I expected Theresa to be a person with depth, and when she stepped into heroism at Etta's side, this time I wasn't surprised.

The Road has almost infinite branches, and Etta, our Queen of the Crossroads, also represents a crossroads for these stories. Piper will continue to travel, and Etta will continue to rule Worldsbridge and explore its secrets. I have more to tell you about both.

As always, I'm grateful for any reader who walks this road with me.

-Erica Anoe, March 2022

ACKNOWLEDGMENTS

Thank you for the Roads you walk, whether they are Roads of words, the Road of life, the Roads in the place you call home or Roads that seem impossibly removed from anything you know. As a writer wandering through the world of words, I'm incredibly grateful whenever a reader joins me here.

Thank you to Elizabeth for the cover and for believing in the Road's Beloved and loving them too. It's hard to overstate how much it matters when someone "gets it," and you always do.

Thank you to Lonely Robot Press for creating a beautiful edition of this story. As someone who's sometimes struggled with the "getting stories out into the world" part of the writing process, I'm incredibly grateful to have a way for readers to find these stories.

Thank you to Dean Wesley Smith. The idea of writing about a view came from Dean, and he also pointed out how much can be done with a story starting from a view. I'm still studying what Dean means when he speaks about depth in writing, but in this story, some of that came together for me. When I put Etta at the window and had her look out at the city where she is Queen, I realized that this view would mean different things to her than it does to anyone else. She sees details that remind her of particular childhood memories, she dreams of seeing a sign of her lost lover, she searches for clues about her place in the world. The truth is that no two people would look at the same view the same way, and this is a breathtaking thing to think about as a writer or reader. The world of story is infinite and thrilling for just this reason, and I'm grateful to Dean for being a wonderful teacher and helping me to see these things and bring them into my writing.

Thank you to Paul. Your belief in who I am as a person and a writer means the world. I couldn't ask for a better Pokemon.

Thank you to the Road, particularly the city roads that have gone into my own understanding of Worldsbridge. I've been privileged to know a few cities fairly deeply, and each one has taught me that a great city's roads can take almost infinite turns. It's amazing how far you can travel even a block from a city apartment, and this absolutely helps me understand what Worldsbridge is and can be.

About the Author

Erica Anoe is a hapa haole writer who is interested in exploring characters and places that exist on the borderlands. Born in Kailua, Hawai'i, she currently lives on the mainland and works in cybersecurity.

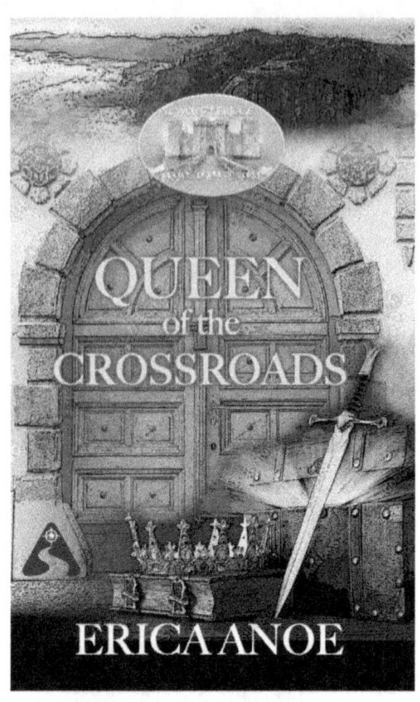

Piper is a Road's Beloved, an eternal traveler who has been given power and destiny by the Road itself. The tangle of birthmarks that cover her skin represent the gifts of every road she has ever walked or will ever walk. They are the source of her magic, and they define her place in the world.

When Piper arrives at Worldsbridge to claim a message from its ruler, she expects a simple encounter. Instead, she finds herself threatened by a bitter king who holds secret grudges against her kind.

To survive, Piper must uncover the true nature of Worldsbridge and learn what the Road expects of those it loves.

"Queen of the Crossroads" is a Road's Beloved short story set in the legendary city of Worldsbridge.

Bridge of Fate

Every night, she dreams of locked doors.

Worldsbridge, the great city where all roads meet, slept for a generation under the rule of a stagnant, mad king. Etta replaced him on Worldsbridge's throne at the command of the spirit of the Road itself, but her fate demands she accomplish even more.

Piper, an immortal traveler who serves the Road, lives a life of leaving. In Worldsbridge, beside Etta, she's finding something that resembles home. The Road, however, is not made for rest.

Together, Piper and Etta must fulfill their destiny and unlock the secret power of Worldsbridge, no matter the personal consequences.

"Bridge of Fate" is a Road's Beloved short story set in the legendary city of Worldsbridge.

Historical Fiction

Trapped in the Hold of the SS Madras: A Kingdom of Hawai'i Short Story

"We were not sick with smallpox, but we knew we would be soon if we couldn't get out of this hold."

April 1883. The SS Madras arrives at the port of Honolulu with hundreds of workers for the rice paddies of Waikiki – but it also carries smallpox. Historical fiction set in the waters of the Kingdom of Hawai'i, "Trapped in the Hold of the SS Madras" tells the story of a steamer mired in uncertainty, a kingdom determined to avoid another plague, and passengers desperate to disembark before they contract a deadly disease.

Includes a historical note by the author with information about the case heard by the Supreme Court of the Kingdom of Hawai'i that inspired this story.

www.ingramcontent.com/pod-product-compliance
Lightning Source LLC
Chambersburg PA
CBHW051936150726
47999CB00006B/2247